The New Adventures of
MARY-KATE & ASHLEY™

The Case Of The
EASTER EGG RACE

Look for more great books in

The New Adventures of
MARY-KATE & ASHLEY ™
series:

The Case Of The
EASTER EGG RACE

by Heather Alexander

📖 HarperEntertainment
An Imprint of HarperCollins*Publishers*

A PARACHUTE PRESS BOOK

PARACHUTE PRESS

Parachute Publishing, L.L.C.
156 Fifth Avenue
New York, NY 10010

DUALSTAR PUBLICATIONS

Dualstar Publications
c/o Thorne and Company
A Professional Law Corporation
1801 Century Park East
Los Angeles, CA 90067

HarperEntertainment

An Imprint of HarperCollins*Publishers*
10 East 53rd Street, New York, NY 10022

For information address HarperCollins Publishers Inc.,
10 East 53rd Street, New York, NY 10022.

ISBN 0-06-009344-7

First printing: March 2004

Printed in the United States of America

ON YOUR MARK, GET SET, GO!

"Hurry up, Mary-Kate!" my twin sister, Ashley, said. "The Easter egg race is about to begin. Let's get to the starting line."

I finished tying the purple laces of my new roller skates. "An Easter egg hunt on roller skates," I said. "How cool is that!"

"Like Rudy always says, 'Everything's more fun on skates!'" Ashley laughed, tucking her strawberry-blond ponytail into her helmet.

Rudy Rizzo is the owner of Rudy's Roller Rink in the Sunny Grove Shopping Plaza. All the kids in our neighborhood skate there. Every year Rudy holds a big Easter egg race in the park. And today was the day of the big race!

"Help!" someone cried. We looked up. Our friend Samantha Samuels was speeding toward us on her skates. She was totally out of control!

"Use your brake!" I shouted.

But it was too late. Samantha lost her balance and tumbled down on the soft grass on the side of the path. Ashley and I helped her up.

Our friend Tim Park zoomed over to us on his skates. He clutched a doughnut in one hand and a chocolate bunny in the other. "Are you okay?" he asked Samantha.

Samantha took a shaky breath. "I think so," she said.

"Want a doughnut?" Tim asked, trying to cheer her up.

"No, thanks," Samantha answered. "I'm not hungry."

"Oh, good! I am!" Tim shoved the doughnut into his mouth and gulped it down.

We all laughed. Tim loves to eat more than anything!

Rainbow Doughnuts, another store in the Sunny Grove Shopping Plaza, was giving out free doughnuts. Patsy's Photo Barn and Bailey's All-Star Talent Agency, two more stores in the plaza, were taking pictures of the race.

Samantha sighed. "I'm not very good at stopping yet. I'm probably the worst skater here."

"No way," said Tim. "You're not the worst skater." He pointed at a brown-haired boy standing next to a bench. "Brett Ellery is much worse than you. You can't stop—but he can't even stand up straight with his skates on!"

We all turned to look. Brett's left foot slid one way. His right foot slid the other way. He grabbed onto the bench and hauled himself up.

When he saw us looking, Brett waved. "Hi, guys!" Suddenly both feet slid out from under him and he fell flat on his butt!

"Whoops!" Brett called as he got back up. Then he bowed, as if he were onstage. Everyone clapped. Brett grinned. His braces sparkled in the sun.

Ashley laughed. "Brett is always putting on a show."

"No wonder he's the star of all our school plays," Samantha said.

Just then our neighbor, Patty O'Leary, skated over to us. "What do you think of my outfit?" she asked. She twirled around in a circle.

Patty had on a pink helmet over her brown hair, a pink-and-white striped T-shirt, a ruffled pink skirt, and pink skates.

"Um . . . it's very . . ." Ashley started to say.

"Pink!" I finished.

Patty put her hands on her hips. "But don't I look pretty?" she asked. "Like a star?"

Ashley and I rolled our eyes. Princess Patty strikes again! We call her "Princess" because she acts like one.

"Did someone say star?" a girl called. "Because *I* am the star of this race!" Casey, a new girl at school, skated up to us.

"Wow," Samantha said. "That sure is a sparkly outfit."

Everything on Casey sparkled. Her roller skates were covered with rainbow glitter. Her name was spelled out in silver glitter across her blue helmet. Even Casey's mouth sparkled! She is the only person in our whole class who wears sparkly braces.

"You should see the awesome dress my mom made for me to wear in Rudy's commercial," Casey said. "It's even more sparkly than what I'm wearing now."

"What are you talking about?" Patty asked.

"The winner of the Easter egg race gets to star in a TV commercial for Rudy's Roller Rink," I reminded her.

Patty tossed her head. "I *know* that." She pointed at Casey. "But why is she talking like she's already won the race?"

Casey skated closer to Patty. "Because you've got to act like a winner to be a winner—and *I am* a winner. That's how I know I'm going to win this race!"

I couldn't stop myself from giggling. If Patty was a princess, then Casey was a queen!

A whistle blew. "Come on, everybody,"

Rudy called. "We're ready to start the race!" He was standing next to a huge oak tree near the entrance to the park. A sign that read START hung on the tree.

"Welcome to the Easter egg race!" Rudy said. He had a shiny bald head, and he wore a polka-dot shirt and a tie that had Easter bunnies printed all over it. "Is everyone ready to skate and have fun?"

"Yes!" we all said.

"First, let me tell you the rules," Rudy continued. "This morning I hid fifteen golden eggs in the park. The eggs look like this." He held up a hard-boiled egg that was painted gold. "Each egg is hidden in a different spot. They are very tricky to find."

"Not for the Trenchcoat Twins," Tim whispered to Ashley and me. "You two can find anything."

Ashley and I smiled. We're detectives. People call us the Trenchcoat Twins. We run the Olsen and Olsen Detective Agency out of the attic of our house.

"But this isn't a mystery, Tim," I said. "Without clues, it won't be easy to find the eggs."

"You will have thirty minutes to find as many eggs as you can," Rudy went on. "If you drop an egg and it cracks, it doesn't count. When you hear the whistle, take all the eggs you have found and skate as fast as you can back to this tree. The winner is the person who gathers the most golden eggs and crosses the finish line first."

"Excuse me," Casey called. "How am I supposed to carry all the eggs I find?"

"I don't believe it," Patty muttered. "She really thinks she's going to find *all* the eggs."

Rudy smiled at Casey. "In your Easter baskets, of course!" Rudy's wife, Mrs. Rizzo, gave us each a basket.

Rudy pointed to a yellow line painted on

the grass near the tree. "Everyone to the starting line."

Skate wheels screeched as we all tried to find a good spot. I squeezed next to Ashley. Adam Milano, a boy in our class, squeezed in next to me.

"Hey!" I said to Adam. "Quit pushing!"

"Sorry, Mary-Kate," Adam said. "I need a good spot if I'm going to win."

Rudy blew his whistle. "On your mark, get set . . . go!"

We all took off as fast as we could.

Ashley and I skated up the main path. Casey zoomed past us. Tim, Samantha, and Patty skated off in different directions.

"Do you see any eggs?" Ashley called.

"No," I called back. "The grass is so high, it's hard to see anything." A group of kids sped by. I turned sideways to get out of their way. I wondered if any of them had found eggs yet.

Ashley pointed to the lake in the center of the meadow. "Let's look over there," she said.

I followed Ashley onto the path that led to the lake. I kept my eyes wide open, trying to spot eggs. I skated around a curve in the road.

"Ooops!" I quickly put my heel up to stop. Brett had fallen on the path, and I almost ran over him! "Are you okay?"

"Yeah, I'm okay," he said. He got to his feet and skated away as best he could.

"Mary-Kate, look!" Ashley called. "It's the Easter bunny!"

Well, it was really a person wearing a fluffy white Easter bunny costume. The bunny darted between the bushes. Its tall ears peeked out from behind the leaves. Then the bunny hopped away down a different path.

Ashley and I giggled.

"I guess the Easter bunny is looking for eggs too," I said.

We sped across the meadow path toward the lake. That's when I saw it. The bright sunshine made it sparkle in the dark green grass.

"I see an egg!" I cried.

AND THE WINNER IS . . .

"**H**ooray!" Ashley cheered. "Go, Mary-Kate, go!"

I raced down the path to the golden egg. It was tucked under a bunch of tulips. I reached out to grab it and . . .

BAM! Someone knocked me over and I fell onto the grass. Out of the corner of my eye, I saw a hand reaching out for the golden egg—*my* golden egg!

"Don't touch that egg!" Ashley cried.

I looked up. Ashley was standing over me with her hands on her hips, glaring at Adam Milano.

"That is Mary-Kate's egg," Ashley told him.

"No way!" Adam cried.

"You *know* she saw it first," Ashley said firmly. She reached out her hand.

Adam looked mad, but he gave Ashley the egg.

"Okay. I guess you can have that one," he said. "But I'm going to get the next one!" He turned and raced down the path.

"Thanks, Ashley," I said. Having a sister is great!

I stood up and brushed the grass from my knee pads. Ashley tucked the egg into my basket.

"Are you *sure* you're okay?" Ashley asked me.

"I'm okay," I said. I pointed to a clump of bushes ahead of us. The Easter bunny's long ears were peeking out. "Look! It's the Easter bunny again. I wonder what it's doing here."

"Maybe Rudy hired the bunny for the race," Ashley said. "Come on. We don't have much time left. Let's go."

Together we sped toward the picnic area of the park. We looked under all the tables and benches. No eggs.

We skated by the big willow tree. No eggs.

We raced to the playground. "I see an egg!" Ashley cried. "Come on, Mary-Kate!"

Ashley zoomed to the side of the swing set. She scooped a golden egg from the grass. The egg gleamed in the sunlight. Ashley placed it safely inside her basket.

"Cool!" I gave my sister a high five. "Now we each have one."

SCREECH! We heard a loud whistle. That meant the race was over!

Ashley and I skated toward the finish line as fast as we could. We crossed it together. Adam, Casey, and Brett were already there.

"Good job, girls," Rudy said.

"Thanks, Rudy!" Ashley said.

I huffed and puffed. I was out of breath.

Samantha, Tim, and Patty skated across the line a few minutes later.

When all the other kids had crossed the finish line, Rudy started counting up the eggs. Then he announced the scores. I had one egg and so did Ashley. Adam had two eggs and so did Brett. Casey had *nine* eggs!

Rudy held Casey's arm up high. "Casey Bailey is the winner!" he called. "She found more eggs than anyone has ever found in the history of the race! She will be the star of the Rudy's Roller Rink commercial!"

Casey bounced around on her skates. "I

knew I'd win!" she screamed. "I knew it! I knew it! I knew it!"

We all clapped. A bunch of kids from our class skated over to us. They did not look happy.

"Look at her," Patty said, pointing at Casey. "She thinks she is so great!"

Casey was posing for a picture with Rudy and the mayor. A tall woman with curly red hair was taking the pictures. She looked just like Casey. I wondered if she was Casey's mother.

"Yeah," Samantha said. "I don't want to sound like a sore loser, but Casey is acting like a sore winner."

"It's not fair," Zach Jones said. "There's no way anyone could find nine eggs! Unless . . ."

"Unless what?" I asked.

BEEP! A car horn honked. Our mom was here to pick us up. Ashley and I waved

good-bye to our friends and skated to the car.

All the way home I wondered what Zach had meant. Unless . . . *what*?

After lunch, Ashley and I headed upstairs to the attic—the headquarters of the Olsen and Olsen Detective Agency. Our silent partner, our basset hound, Clue, was snoozing on the couch. We sat down and started making Easter baskets for our little sister, Lizzie.

Suddenly there was a knock on the door.

"Quick, hide everything! It's Lizzie!" Ashley whispered. We shoved our baskets, the decorations, and the bags of chocolate eggs under our side-by-side desks.

"Come in!" I called.

The door burst open.

It wasn't Lizzie. It was Casey—and she was crying!

"Mary-Kate! Ashley! I need your help!" Casey said. "Rudy says I cheated in the race and now I can't be in the commercial!" She sniffed. "But I didn't cheat! And I want you guys to prove it!"

THE MISSING MAP

Ashley and I stared at Casey. Tears spilled down her cheeks. Her face was red and blotchy. There was nothing sparkly about her now.

I led Casey over to one of our desk chairs. "Sit down and tell us exactly what happened," I said.

Ashley opened her detective notebook to a blank page. She always takes lots of notes when we have a case to solve. It's important to write down all the facts so we don't forget anything later. Our great-grandma Olive taught us that. She is a detective too.

Casey took a deep breath. "I won the race. You saw—you were there! After I got my picture taken with Rudy, Mrs. Rizzo came over. She told Rudy that someone stole the Easter egg map from his desk drawer at the roller rink."

"What Easter egg map?" Ashley asked.

"Rudy had a supersecret map that he used to hide the eggs in the park," Casey explained, "so he could pick up the eggs after the race just in case we didn't find all of them."

"Why do they think you stole it?" I asked.

"Because I found nine eggs so fast," Casey said.

"That's not enough of a reason to accuse you of stealing," Ashley said.

"I know! But there's something else. . . ." Casey bit her lip. "Mrs. Rizzo said that she saw me at the roller rink this morning before the race."

Ashley stopped writing. "Were you there?"

Casey nodded. "I was thirsty," she explained. "Rudy has the best sports drinks in his vending machines."

"Did you tell him that?" I asked.

"Yes, but Rudy didn't believe me! He said he's going to have another race next weekend and someone else will get to star in the commercial!" Casey burst into loud sobs. "Please—you have to help me prove that I won fair and square!"

Ashley and I looked at each other. We had never seen Casey so upset.

"So are you going to take my case?" she demanded. "All the kids at school say you're good detectives."

Ashley nodded. "We'll take the case," I said.

"Oh, good!" Casey said. "You have to solve it fast, okay? I want to star in that commercial."

"We'll start right away," I said.

"Great!" Casey bent down and grabbed a chocolate egg that had rolled out from under our desks. "Can I have this?" she asked. "I love chocolate."

"Sure," Ashley said, even though Casey had already popped the chocolate into her mouth.

"Thanks! Bye!" Casey hurried out of the room. We heard the front door slam.

"What do we do first?" I asked Ashley.

"Tomorrow we'll talk to Rudy," Ashley said.

On Monday afternoon Ashley and I met at the bike rack at the side of our school.

We unlocked our bikes and pedaled to the roller rink.

All day long the kids at school had been whispering about Casey cheating in the Easter egg race. I felt bad for her.

We turned our bikes into the Sunny Grove Shopping Plaza. Rudy's Roller Rink was at the far right side of the parking lot. We locked up our bikes and headed for the rink. Rudy and his wife were in the lobby when we entered.

"Mary-Kate! Ashley!" Rudy cried, happy to see us. "Are you here to skate?"

"Not today," Ashley said. "We're here on a case. We're trying to find out about the missing Easter egg map."

Rudy's big smile turned into a frown. "Casey stole my map. She cheated to win the race."

Ashley pulled her detective notebook out of her backpack and turned to a new page.

"How do you know it was Casey?" I asked.

"She was at the rink yesterday morning," Rudy said. "The map was in the desk drawer in my office before Casey came in. She left—and then my wife saw it was missing."

"Does Casey skate here a lot?" I asked.

"All the time," Mrs. Rizzo said. "She likes to skate in the middle of the rink, so I always see her."

"Will you show us where you kept the map?" Ashley asked.

Rudy nodded. "Of course."

Rudy and his wife led us to a small office in the back of the arena. A large desk and a chair were in the middle of the room. I saw right away that the office had no windows. That meant that the person who had taken the map came in through the door.

Rudy opened the top left drawer of his desk. "This is where I put the map after I used it to hide the eggs," he said. "Then I went back to the park to start the race."

"I was working in the office after Rudy left," Mrs. Rizzo said. "Then I went out to get some doughnuts. Someone must have taken the map while I was gone. I didn't find out it was missing until after the race."

"Is it okay if we look around?" I asked.

"Go ahead," Rudy said.

Ashley and I slowly made our way around the room. We were looking for clues—anything that the person who took the map had left behind or moved out of place.

We didn't find anything.

Ashley turned to Rudy and his wife. "Is this how the room looked yesterday morning?" she asked. "Does anything look different?"

They looked closely around the room.

"Wait!" cried Mrs. Rizzo. "Yes! I see something!"

4

THE HEADLESS BUNNY

"**W**hat do you see that's different?" I asked.

Mrs. Rizzo pointed to a brown lump sitting on the corner of the large desk. "That wasn't here yesterday."

I peered at the lump. "What is it?"

"It looks like a chocolate bunny," Ashley said.

"It *is* a chocolate bunny," I said. I held up the candy. The foil wrapper only covered the lower half of the bunny. "Someone bit off its head!"

"That's not mine," Mrs. Rizzo said.

"Or mine," Rudy said. "And we don't sell those here."

"The thief must have left it behind," I said. "Can we keep it as evidence?"

"Sure," said Rudy.

Ashley pulled a small plastic bag from her backpack. I carefully placed the chocolate inside the bag.

"Let's go over what we know so far," Ashley said. "First, the thief likes chocolate."

I laughed. "Almost *everyone* likes chocolate, Ashley!"

"That's true," Ashley said. She went on. "Second, the thief knew when Mrs. Rizzo was out of the office. And third, the thief knew there was a secret map that showed where the eggs were hidden!"

"Good thinking, Ashley!" I said.

Ashley turned to Rudy. "Who else knew about the map?"

"Well, let me see now . . . " Rudy said, scratching his head.

"Jacob knew about the map," Mrs. Rizzo said. "He sells the tickets in the booth up front."

Ashley wrote Jacob's name down in her notebook.

Rudy snapped his fingers. "All the other store owners in the Sunny Grove Shopping Plaza knew about the map too. They helped me pay for the race."

"Thanks, Rudy! Thanks, Mrs. Rizzo!" Ashley said. She grabbed my arm. "Come on, Mary-Kate. Let's go talk to Jacob."

We found Jacob inside the ticket booth near the vending machines. He took our tickets whenever we came to the rink to go skating. But he never said very much.

"Hi, Jacob!" I said.

Jacob looked up from the comic book he was reading. "You girls want a ticket?" he asked.

Ashley shook her head. "No," she said. "We were just wondering . . . do you work here every day?"

Jacob stared at us with sleepy brown eyes. Finally he said, "Yeah. So what?"

"Were you here yesterday morning?" I asked.

"Yeah . . ."

"Did anyone besides Casey come into the rink yesterday morning before the race?" I asked.

"No." Jacob yawned.

I was having a hard time talking to Jacob. He was making me sleepy. "Your turn," I whispered to Ashley.

Ashley smiled at Jacob and pointed to the vending machines. "I have some extra quarters. Do you want to share a chocolate bar?"

What is Ashley up to? I wondered.

"Nope," he said.

Ashley looked hurt. "Why not?"

"Don't like chocolate," Jacob said.

"Oh, well, thanks anyway," Ashley said. "Let's go, Mary-Kate." She rushed out of the rink. I had to hurry to keep up with her.

Outside, in the warm afternoon sun, Ashley flipped open her notebook. She put an *X* through Jacob's name.

"He doesn't like chocolate, so he didn't bite the head off the chocolate bunny and leave it on Rudy's desk," she said. "So he's not the thief."

"Good going, Ashley," I said. "Now let's talk to the other store owners who knew about the map."

I squinted into the sun and looked at

the stores in the shopping plaza. I read the signs out loud: "'Rainbow Doughnuts. Patsy's Photo Barn. Bailey's All-Star Talent Agency.'"

"Wait a second," Ashley said. "Isn't Casey's last name Bailey?"

"You're right," I said slowly. I had a funny feeling in my stomach. "Do you think Casey's family has a store right next to Rudy's Roller Rink? And that Casey knew about the map?"

"Let's go find out!"

Ashley and I hurried to the door of Bailey's All-Star Talent Agency. A huge poster hung on the door. "'Want to be a TV or movie star? Come inside and we'll make your dreams come true,'" I read.

"I guess they help get people on TV or in the movies," Ashley said, opening the door.

We stepped into a large waiting room . . . and saw Casey!

Casey turned around. "The Trenchcoat Twins are here!" she exclaimed. "Did you solve my case yet?"

"Not yet," I said, looking around. There were lots of framed photographs decorating the walls.

"What's taking so long?" Casey demanded.

"Finding clues takes time," Ashley said.

A door at the far end of the room burst open. A red-headed woman hurried out. She was the woman I had seen taking pictures of Casey at the race!

"Mom," Casey said, "this is Mary-Kate, and this is Ashley. They're the ones helping me."

Mrs. Bailey smiled at us. "Hello, girls," she said. Before we could answer, she started talking really fast. "Can you believe they took the commercial away from my Casey? They are wrong, so wrong. My Casey is a star. She's been a star since she

was born. This is her big chance to shine. She needs this commercial!"

Wow! Mrs. Bailey sure wants Casey to star in that commercial! I thought.

Ashley took a deep breath. "Mrs. Bailey," she said, "Rudy said that you were one of the people he told about the Easter egg map."

"Yes, I knew about the map," she said.

"Did you tell Casey there was a map?" I asked.

Casey's mom fluffed up her short red hair. "No, of course not!"

"Mom!" Casey wailed. "You did so tell me about the map!"

5

COULD IT BE CASEY?

Mrs. Bailey turned red. "I did?" she said. "Oh, well, I guess I must have forgotten." She looked down at her nails.

"Mom, I told you Mary-Kate and Ashley would fix everything!" Casey said. "You can tell them the truth!"

"But, honey, I don't want you to get into any more trouble," Mrs. Bailey said.

Casey turned to us. "I did know about the map, but I didn't steal it! Please, oh *please*, you have to believe me!" She started to cry. "You have to get that commercial back for me! You will, won't you?"

"Uh . . . sure," Ashley said. Only she didn't *look* very sure. "We're going to look for clues now." She grabbed my hand, and we left the talent agency—fast.

"I don't get it," Ashley said. She twirled a few strands of her strawberry-blond hair. "Everything we find out makes me think that Casey did cheat."

"I think so too," I said. "Casey knew there was a map. She was the only one at the roller rink before the race. And she *really* wants to be in the commercial."

"And she loves chocolate," Ashley reminded me. "Remember? She took that chocolate egg when we were in our office."

"Do you think Casey is lying to us?" I asked.

Ashley shook her head. "We can't think

that way. It's not fair. We have no real proof that Casey stole the map."

"Okay," I said, "but I think we should still write her name down as a suspect."

Ashley opened her notebook and wrote SUSPECT #1: CASEY BAILEY.

"Let's go talk to the other people who knew about the map," Ashley said. She pointed to Rainbow Doughnuts at the far end of the shopping plaza. "Doughnuts first."

The air inside the doughnut store smelled sugary. I took a deep breath. I love that smell!

A teenage boy was standing behind the counter. As Ashley asked him about the map, I stared at the pink frosting on my favorite kind of doughnut. My mouth watered.

"Sure, Rudy told me about the map," the boy said.

"Did you tell anyone?" Ashley asked.

"One person," the boy said. "My neigh-

bor. He was in here right before the race buying doughnuts."

I made myself look at the boy instead of at the doughnuts. "Who is your neighbor?" I asked.

"Adam Milano," he said.

My eyes opened wide. "Thanks!" I hurried out the door after Ashley.

Outside the store Ashley was already writing in her notebook SUSPECT #2: ADAM MILANO.

"He was trying really hard to get the golden eggs," Ashley said. "Remember how he pushed you?"

"Yes." I showed Ashley the black-and-blue mark on my leg. "Look! I still have the bruise! Let's go talk to Adam."

Ashley pointed to the photo store next to the doughnut shop. "Right after we check out Patsy's Photo Barn."

I dashed over and tried the door. It was

locked. All the lights in the store were off.

"It's closed," I told Ashley.

"Mary-Kate! Ashley!"

I whirled around. Brett was standing by a car in the parking lot. We went over to say hi. An older girl was sitting in the driver's seat. She acted as if she didn't see us.

"Hi, Brett," I said.

"What are you two doing here?" he asked.

"We're working on a case," Ashley said.

He laughed. "Is that for real? Some guys at school said Casey hired you to prove she won the race fair and square. I didn't believe it."

"It's true," Ashley said. "What's wrong with that?"

Brett shrugged. "Nothing, I guess. But I'm sure Casey cheated to win the race. I mean, *everyone* thinks so."

"Jacob!" the girl in the car called out her

window. She opened the car door and hurried to the front of the roller rink. Jacob had just come outside.

Brett rolled his eyes. "That's my sister, Julia. She *really* likes Jacob. They always talk forever. I'm going to be waiting here for a long time!"

"We have to get home," I said to Brett. "See you at school." Ashley and I got our bikes. I waved to Brett as we pedaled away down the street.

When we got home, I took the plastic bag with the headless chocolate bunny and taped a sign to it: DO NOT EAT! EVIDENCE! Then I put the bag in the refrigerator. I didn't want the chocolate to melt.

I closed the refrigerator. The door was covered with Easter cards our mom had taped to it. The card from Great-Grandma Olive had a big Easter bunny on it. *Easter bunny!* Suddenly, an idea popped into my head.

"Ashley," I called, "come and look at this!"

Ashley came and stood beside me. "Nice card," she said.

"No—the Easter bunny," I said. "Remember the Easter bunny at the race?"

"What about it?" Ashley asked, still confused.

"The Easter bunny was all over the park during the race. Maybe whoever was in the costume saw someone cheating," I said.

Ashley's face lit up. "Great idea, Mary-Kate! Let's call Rudy right now!"

We raced to our attic office and called Rudy on the telephone.

"Who was the Easter bunny you hired for the race?" I asked him.

"Easter bunny?" Rudy said. "What Easter bunny? I never hired a bunny!"

6

BUNNIES, BUNNIES EVERYWHERE

I hung up the phone and turned to Ashley. "Rudy says he didn't hire the bunny," I told her. "This case is getting weirder and weirder!"

"Maybe the Easter bunny has something to do with the case," Ashley said.

"Yes, but what?" I couldn't think of anything. I sighed.

Ashley pulled out her detective notebook and wrote EASTER BUNNY? on a blank page. Then she turned to the list of suspects. "We still have to talk to Adam," she said. "He knew about the map."

"We can talk to him tomorrow at school," I said. "Let's try to find the Easter bunny now."

"How are we going to do that?" Ashley asked. "It's not like there's a listing in the phone book for *Easter bunny*."

I smiled. "Yes, there is." I turned on my computer and typed in the address of the Internet yellow pages. I used it to find the names of the costume stores in our town. There were three stores listed.

"Great thinking, Mary-Kate," Ashley said. "The Easter bunny must have rented the costume from a store."

She picked up the phone and dialed the number of the first store. They didn't own an Easter bunny costume.

Ashley called the second store. They did

have an Easter bunny costume, but they had sent it to a school all the way in Texas.

There was no answer at the third store.

"What now?" Ashley asked.

"Hey, Mary-Kate! Hey, Ashley!" called a girl's voice from outside our house. Ashley and I looked out the window. Samantha and Tim were riding their scooters in the street. They waved for us to come down.

We ran downstairs. Samantha and Tim rested their scooters by the curb and we all sat down on our lawn.

"We thought we'd come over and see how you're doing on the case," Samantha said.

"Yeah! Do you need any help?" Tim asked.

Samantha and Tim love helping us on our cases.

"Do you remember seeing an Easter bunny during the race in the park?" I asked Tim.

"Yes!" Tim said. "I thought it was funny."

"I saw it too," Samantha said.

"Who was wearing the costume?" Ashley asked.

"I don't know," Samantha said. "Do you?" she asked Tim.

"No idea," said Tim. He reached into his pocket and pulled out something wrapped in shiny foil. He peeled off the foil and took a bite. I stared at him.

Tim looked up and saw me watching. "Want some?" he asked.

I reached out my hand. Tim gave me a chocolate bunny. It was exactly the same kind of chocolate bunny that we'd found in Rudy's office!

"Where did you get this?" I asked Tim.

"Adam gave it to me," he said.

7

FUNNY BUNNY BUSINESS

We didn't waste any time. Ashley and I ran straight to Adam's house. He lived only a few blocks away. When we got there, Adam was in the front yard. He was dribbling a soccer ball.

"Hi! What's up?" he asked.

"We're working on a case," Ashley said. "Can we ask you some questions?"

Adam stopped dribbling. He looked surprised. "Okay," he said.

"Have you ever seen this chocolate bunny before?" I asked. I showed him the bunny.

"Yeah, I gave one just like it to Tim. Why?" he asked.

"Well, we found one just like it on Rudy's desk at the roller rink," Ashley said.

"The cheater who took the Easter egg map for the race left it there," I added.

"Hold on! I didn't take the map!" Adam cried.

"But you did know about the map before the race, right?" Ashley asked. "The boy in the doughnut store told us you did."

Adam shoved his hands into his pockets. "Just because I knew about the map doesn't mean I stole it. Besides, I didn't even want to be in that dopey commercial."

"Really?" I said. "Why not?"

"I'd be too scared to be on TV."

"Then why were you trying so hard to win the race?" Ashley asked.

"I had a bet with Tim. I said I would find more eggs than he would," Adam said. "I didn't win, so I had to give Tim three chocolate bunnies."

"That's too bad," I said. "Where did you get the chocolate bunnies?"

"My mom brought a bag of them home from the candy store last week," Adam said. "Do you want one? We have a lot of them in the kitchen."

Ashley shook her head.

"No, thanks," I said. "Bye."

We headed for home. The sun was going down.

Ashley said, "Do you believe Adam?"

"I guess so. Do you?"

"I think he was telling the truth, but I'm not sure," she said. "I don't think we can cross him off our suspect list yet."

"Yeah, there's no way we can prove that Adam was the one who left the chocolate bunny in Rudy's office," I said. I sighed.

Ashley stopped walking. "Wait a second!" she cried. "Yes there is!"

"How?" I asked.

"Teeth prints!" Ashley said. "The chocolate bunny has teeth marks where someone took a bite, right?"

I nodded. "Right."

"Maybe teeth marks can identify a person the same way fingerprints can," Ashley said.

Ashley and I have solved a lot of our other cases with fingerprints. We match fingerprints that were left at a scene of the crime to the person who did it.

"You could be right," I said. "And I know just the person who can help us tomorrow!"

Ashley grinned. "We're getting closer and closer to solving this case. I know it!"

• • •

As soon as the bell rang at the end of school on Tuesday, Ashley and I hopped on our bikes and went to see our dentist, Dr. Sperling.

"Hello, girls," he said. He looked surprised to see us. We didn't have an appointment. "What's wrong? Toothache? Loose tooth?"

"No, everything is fine!" I covered my mouth with my hands. I didn't want him to get any ideas!

Ashley told him all about our case and her idea that the teeth marks on the chocolate bunny could help us find the person who stole the Easter egg map.

I pulled the plastic bag with the chocolate bunny in it out of my backpack and showed it to Dr. Sperling.

Dr. Sperling nodded. "Detectives often use teeth prints to find criminals," he said. "Your teeth always leave marks when you bite down on something."

"How do you tell one person's teeth from another's?" I asked. I pointed to my sister. "Ashley's teeth look just like mine."

"That's where you are wrong!" Dr. Sperling said. "Everyone's teeth are different. Some people have a lot of space between their teeth. Some people's teeth are very close together."

He reached for several sets of fake teeth on his shelf. "Some teeth have chips. Some teeth are crooked. Some teeth are missing. Some people have more teeth than other people."

I pulled a magnifying glass out of my backpack and handed it to Dr. Sperling. "Do the teeth marks in this chocolate bunny tell you anything?" I asked.

He studied the chocolate. "The person who bit the head off this bunny has all of his or her teeth. There are no empty spaces between the teeth."

"Adam is missing his front tooth," I reminded Ashley, "so it's not him."

Dr. Sperling smiled. "The person who bit this had something special about his or her teeth. Come with me, girls."

We followed Dr. Sperling into his office. He opened a cabinet and pulled out two chocolate bars. "My secret hiding place," he said with a wink. He handed the candy to us. "Take a bite."

Ashley and I bit into our chocolate bars. We looked at our teeth marks. Then we looked at the marks on the bunny. The teeth marks on the bunny looked really different from ours. They looked kind of bumpy.

"Braces!" I said. "The person who ate the chocolate bunny was wearing braces, right?"

"Right," Dr. Sperling said.

Ashley and I looked at each another. Casey wears braces! Sparkly ones!

8

ON THE BUNNY TRAIL

The minute we left Dr. Sperling's office, I blurted out, "Casey stole the map and cheated to win the race. Case closed!"

Ashley didn't say anything.

"I can't believe it!" I said. "Casey—the person who hired us to *find* the cheater—*is* the cheater!"

"I don't think we should close the case," Ashley said.

"Come on, Ashley!" I said. "We have

proof! A chocolate bunny bitten by some-one with braces. Casey has braces. And she was in the roller rink that morning."

"Other kids have braces too," Ashley said. "We need more proof."

I sighed. Ashley was right. She is a good detective. She always makes sure the pieces of a case fit together exactly—just like in a puzzle.

"What kind of proof do we need?" I asked.

Ashley shrugged. "I don't know. I mean, if we found Casey holding the map, then—"

"I've got it!" I cut in. "Follow me!" I raced down the street. "We've got to call Rudy!"

I hurried to our house. I ran up the stairs to our attic office two at a time. Ashley was right behind me.

I grabbed the telephone and dialed Rudy's number. Ashley listened in.

Rudy answered the phone. "Hello, Rudy's Roller Rink," he said.

"Could you help us with something for the case?" I asked Rudy. "We need evidence to prove that the person we think took the map really did!"

"Who do you think took it?" Rudy asked.

I bit my lip. "I can't say yet." I knew it wasn't right to tell Rudy that we thought it was Casey. Not until we had proof.

"Okay. What do you need me to do?" Rudy asked.

"Can you make a new map and tell the same people you told about the map last time that you made a new map for the new race?" I said.

"Sure," Rudy said. "I'll do it tonight. I need to make a new map for next week's race anyway."

I thanked him and hung up the phone.

The plan was going to work!

"What was that about?" Ashley asked.

"All we have to do is follow Casey tomorrow afternoon," I said. "If she took the map the first time, I'm sure she'll try to take the map again. We'll catch her, and then we'll have proof."

It was Wednesday afternoon, and school was over for the day. Ashley and I peeked out from our hiding place near the front door of the school. We were waiting for Casey to show up.

Finally we saw her! She walked out the door and turned left outside the school yard. Ashley and I waited until Casey was halfway down the street, then we followed her.

"We have to make sure she doesn't see us," I said.

Ashley nodded.

We kept a few feet behind Casey. I could hear the *clop*, *clop* of her glittery clogs as she walked. When she turned right, we turned right. When she turned left, we turned left.

"Where is she going?" Ashley whispered. "Her house is the other way."

"I know where she's going!" I said. "This is the way to Rudy's Roller Rink!"

Ashley gasped. "Do you think she's going to steal the new map?"

"I knew it was her!" I said.

We followed Casey until we were almost at the roller rink. Suddenly Casey stopped and turned around.

Oh, no! We ducked behind a parked car in the Sunny Grove Shopping Plaza parking lot. I pressed myself against the tire of the car and waited. My heart beat loudly. *Did she see us?* I wondered.

Finally we heard the *clop, clop* of Casey's clogs. She was walking away.

"That was close," Ashley whispered.

We slowly stood up. I watched Casey walk across the parking lot. If she went into the roller rink, our case was closed for sure!

I held my breath, waiting to see where Casey would go. She opened the door to Bailey's All-Star Talent Agency and disappeared inside.

I shook my head. "That didn't work out like I thought it would. What should we do now?" I asked Ashley.

"Let's go see Rudy," she said.

I followed her through the glass door and into the lobby of the rink. Jacob was sitting in the ticket booth.

"Hi," he said. "Got any more questions for me?"

"Not today," I said.

Rudy spotted us and hurried over. "I made a new map," he told us. He pulled a folded piece of paper from his back pocket.

"And I told everyone about it, just like you asked me to."

"Does that map show where all the golden eggs will be hidden for the new race?" Ashley asked.

"Yes," Rudy said, tucking the map back into his pocket. He waved a finger at us and grinned. "Don't peek. I want you both to be in my new race."

"We'll be there," I said, smiling.

Rudy sighed. "Having a second race is a lot of work. I need more waterproof gold paint for the new eggs. I have to drive all the way to the art store on the highway now."

"What about the art store in town?" Ashley said.

"I went there already. Two girls came in before me and bought all of the gold paint." Rudy pulled his car keys out of his pocket and hurried toward his red car. "Bye, girls."

Ashley tugged my shirtsleeve. "Casey is leaving." She pointed out the glass door.

I could see Casey walking across the parking lot. She was carrying a large plastic shopping bag and heading toward the sidewalk. Ashley and I ran after her.

"Which way did she go?" I asked Ashley. I couldn't see Casey anywhere.

Ashley looked both ways. She pointed to a road on the right. "That way. I hear her clogs."

I saw the back of Casey's pink shirt. Her shopping bag was filled with something lumpy. *What's in there?* I wondered. The bag looked heavy.

"What should we do now?" Ashley asked. "Casey never went into the roller rink. She didn't try to take the map."

"I know," I said, "but we should still find out what Casey is up to. I want to know what's in that shopping bag."

We followed Casey up Birch Street all the way to her house. She let herself in the front door. We crept around the side of her house into the backyard.

I could see a light on in a window at the back of the house. Ashley and I crept up to the window.

"It doesn't seem right to peek into her house," Ashley whispered. "It's like spying."

"One quick look to see what's in that bag. Then we're out of here," I said.

I raised my head slowly until I could see into the room. It was the kitchen. Casey was sitting at the kitchen table.

"What is she doing?" Ashley whispered.

I tried to see. "I think she's painting," I said. "She's painting Easter eggs." I started to move away from the window. Ashley stopped me.

"She's painting Easter eggs *gold*!" Ashley whispered.

My mouth fell open. "Maybe she's painting her eggs to look like Rudy's golden eggs."

"I get it!" Ashley said. "Then Casey can say she found a lot of golden eggs at the new race, but they will really be the eggs that she painted!"

"She's going to cheat again!" I said. "What should we do?"

9

CAUGHT!

At that moment the back door flew open.

Casey stood in the doorway, her hands on her hips. "Mary-Kate! Ashley! Why are you looking in my window?"

"We . . . uh . . . um . . ." Ashley began.

"We came by and we were wondering what you were doing," I said. Okay, maybe it wasn't the *whole* truth, but I didn't want to call her a cheater yet.

Casey looked confused. "I was painting Easter eggs." She pointed to the eggs and the fancy basket on the table. "My mom boiled a whole bunch for me."

"Why gold?" Ashley asked. "I usually dye my eggs pink or purple."

Casey held up the fancy basket. It glittered. Silver and gold ribbon was woven through the handle.

"This is for Patty," she said. "Patty says that *she* makes the fanciest Easter baskets. *Ha!* My basket is going to be the most sparkly Easter basket ever. Gold eggs make it even more sparkly, don't they?"

"They do," I said. "It's beautiful."

Ashley tugged my arm. "We've got to go, Casey. See you in school tomorrow!"

Once we were away from Casey's house, Ashley turned to me. "Remember when Rudy said that *two* girls bought all of the gold paint? Casey was one of the girls.

But who do you think the other one was?"

"Who else is on our list of suspects?" I asked. Ashley took out her notebook. We looked at the list.

"Casey is still a suspect," she said, "but we crossed Adam off the list."

"You're right. And what about that Easter bunny?" I pointed to the list of costume shops in her notebook. "I'm not sure how, but I think the Easter bunny is part of this case. We never checked out the third costume shop."

Ashley looked at the address in her notebook. "It's not too far from here. We should go now."

The costume store was a tiny place called All Dressed Up. We pushed open the creaky door.

The small space was overflowing with costumes. There were costumes for princesses, pirates, monsters, and all kinds of other creatures. An old woman stood behind a dusty counter. She was sewing a red nose onto an old clown mask.

"Do you have an Easter bunny costume?" Ashley asked her.

"Yes. It's the best Easter bunny costume in town." The woman smiled. "Sorry, girls, but it's rented out."

"Who rented it?" I asked.

"Oh, I can't tell you that," the woman said, making a knot in her thread. "It wouldn't be right." She cut the thread. Then she placed her needle and the clown mask on top of a large book on the counter. I could see names written on the book's lined paper.

"That's okay," Ashley told the woman. She grabbed my hand. "We'll just look around for a costume."

"What costume?" I whispered once we were on the other side of the store.

"No costume," Ashley said. "We have to find a way to look at that book on the counter. I think it has the names of the people who rented costumes."

I nodded. "We need to get that woman away from the counter first."

"I'll do it," Ashley whispered. "You get ready to look at the book."

I moved toward the front of the store. "Excuse me! Excuse me!" I heard Ashley call from the back. "Can you help me get that purple wig?"

"Which wig?" the woman asked. She walked around the counter and headed toward Ashley.

"The one on the very top shelf," Ashley said as I slipped behind the counter. The woman didn't see me.

I quickly lifted the clown mask off the big book. Ashley was right! The book was a list of the costumes that had been rented.

I bent over the book. The handwriting was tiny and messy. I had trouble reading it.

Genie. Knight. Three-headed monster. I looked down the list. *Where is the Easter bunny?*

"Can I see the green wig too?" I heard Ashley ask. I knew I didn't have a lot of time.

I ran my finger down the page. No Easter bunny.

I turned back a page. The paper crinkled loudly. I held my breath, but the woman was still helping Ashley.

Then I saw it on the third line down— *Easter bunny.*

I moved my finger across the line. The costume was rented by—

"Can I help you?" the woman called, hurrying toward the counter.

I looked down at the book. The bunny costume was rented by someone named Julia Ellery.

Julia! I thought. *Brett's big sister!*

"What are you doing back here?" the woman asked, coming around the counter.

I reached for the clown mask. "Can I get this mask?"

The woman shook her head. "No, I need to finish fixing it. But I do have other clown masks." She turned around to reach for a box on the shelf above her.

"I'll have to think about it," I said.

I met Ashley at the door as the woman turned back around. "Bye!" we called as we left.

"What did you find out?" Ashley asked.

I told her about Julia. "The book says Julia rented the costume for Patsy's Photo Barn!"

"Patsy's Photo Barn!" Ashley said. "That's right next to the roller rink!"

10

THE EGG-CITING FINISH

We headed back to the Sunny Grove Shopping Plaza. We were almost done solving the case.

Patsy's Photo Barn was filled with little kids and their mothers. Kids were crying and whining. Mothers were trying to get them to smile.

At the far end of the store, I saw the Easter bunny—the same Easter bunny we had seen at the race at the park. The bunny was sitting on a tall silver throne. A little girl was sitting on its knee. A woman took their picture.

I looked around the crowded store. "We need to talk to the Easter bunny. Let's get in line." I pointed to the velvet ropes that shaped the line of kids. Ashley nodded.

We stood behind a girl in a puffy white dress. She was wearing an Easter bonnet with flowers on it. The girl reached into a big basket sitting on the floor by the velvet rope. A sign on the basket read: TAKE ONE WHILE YOU WAIT. I heard the crinkle of foil.

Suddenly the girl's mother screamed, "Katie, look what you've done to your dress!" The white dress had chocolate fingerprints on it.

I looked into the basket. It was filled with chocolate bunnies wrapped in foil. "Look, Ashley! They're the same kind of chocolate bunny we found in Rudy's office!"

Ashley gave me a thumbs-up. Now we knew we were on the right trail.

The line was moving slowly. It would be a long time before we could talk to the Easter bunny.

"Stay here, okay?" I told Ashley. "I'm going to look around some more."

I walked around the store. In the back, I spotted a bathroom. The door was open. I peeked inside.

A paintbrush lay on the sink. I picked it up. The bristles had gold paint on them. It looked like the same gold paint that Casey had been using to paint her eggs.

I grabbed the paintbrush and hurried back to Ashley. She was near the front of the line.

"Look!" I said, showing her the gold paintbrush. "I think Julia Ellery was the other girl who bought gold paint."

The Easter bunny looked up and saw us.

The bunny hopped up from the throne, whispered something to the photographer, and then disappeared through a door behind the throne.

"The Easter bunny is taking a break," the photographer told everyone.

"Don't let her get away!" Ashley cried. We raced for the door and pushed it open.

In the little room, sitting at a table, was Brett Ellery. And on the table in front of him were fifteen freshly painted gold eggs. The Easter bunny stood next to the table. The bunny lifted off the head of the costume—and inside the costume was Julia!

Brett jumped up. "What are you two doing here?" He didn't look very happy to see us.

"Brett, will you open your mouth, please?" Ashley said.

"Huh?" Brett looked confused. "Why do you want me to open my mouth?"

Something silver flashed inside Brett's mouth. I gasped. "Ashley! Brett wears braces!" I smacked my forehead. How could I forget something like that?

"So?" Brett asked. "I wear braces. Big deal."

"Did you eat a chocolate bunny and leave it in Rudy's office?" Ashley asked.

Brett's face turned red. He looked down at the ground.

"I know," I said. "Jacob from the roller rink told your sister Julia about the Easter egg map, right?"

Brett looked up. "Yeah," he admitted. "Jacob told my sister where the map was, and she told me."

"You stole the map, Brett!" I said. Brett looked away from me. "But why?"

"I really wanted to win the race so I could be in the commercial," Brett said.

"Enough to cheat?" Ashley asked.

"I'm the best actor in our school," Brett said, "but I'm the worst at sports. I knew I couldn't win a roller skating race by myself, so I begged Julia to help me."

"But even with the map, you didn't win," Julia pointed out. "After all the trouble I went to!" She turned to us. "I wore my Easter bunny costume to the race so no one would know who I was. I tried to help Brett by hopping ahead to point out where the eggs were hidden."

"But Casey was way too fast for me," Brett said.

I pointed to the gold eggs on the table. "You were going to cheat again. This time you were going to pretend you found the golden eggs, but use these eggs instead."

Brett and Julia nodded. They both looked embarrassed.

"*Now* the case is closed," Ashley said.

• • •

"It's on!" I called.

Ashley hurried into our living room and plopped down next to me on the sofa. I pointed the remote control at the TV and turned up the volume.

"She looks . . . sparkly," Ashley said.

We watched Casey on TV as she spun around in a circle in the center of Rudy's Roller Rink. She was wearing a dress covered with glitter and her sparkly roller skates.

"I'm glad Rudy didn't have the second race," I said.

"I'm glad he said he was sorry to Casey when we told him it was Brett and Julia who cheated. She really did win fair and square," Ashley said.

"Look how nice the roller rink looks," I said. "Brett had to paint the whole entry-way for making so much trouble for Rudy."

The commercial ended, and I clicked off the TV.

"I'm hungry," Ashley said.

"Me too!" I said. "And I know just what we should have!"

I jumped up and went into the kitchen. I brought back a large bowl of hard-boiled eggs. All the shells were painted gold.

"Want an egg?" I asked.

Ashley laughed. "Eggs-cellent idea!"

Hi from both of us,

Ashley and I entered our basset hound, Clue, in her first-ever dog show. We were so excited when she won the Best of Breed contest. Now Clue would get to compete in the Best in Show contest—and everyone said she was sure to win that too! But right before the Best in Show contest, someone stole Clue!

We had to track down the thief who stole Clue fast—or we might never see our silent partner again! Want to find out what happened? Turn the page for a sneak peek at *The New Adventures of Mary-Kate & Ashley: The Case Of The Dog Show Mystery*.

See you next time!

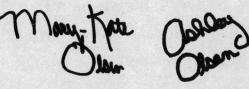

A sneak peek at our next mystery...

The Case Of The
DOG SHOW MYSTERY

"Mary-Kate, look!" My twin sister, Ashley, shook the *Dog Show News* in front of my face.

"I can't see anything with you jiggling it around like that," I said.

Ashley held the newspaper still. On the front page, I saw the sweet face of our basset hound, Clue, staring back at me. I read the headline out loud: "'Newcomer Clue Olsen is the favorite to win the Best in Show competition!'"

I gave Ashley a high five. "Let's go show this to Clue!" Clue was waiting for us backstage in her pen.

"Don't get too excited," a girl called from behind us. We turned around. Deanna and her dalmatian, Darling, flounced over to us. "Newbies never win Best in Show."

"We've got to get inside, Deanna," Ashley said. "We want to get in some last-minute grooming before the show."

I knew what Ashley really wanted to do was get away from Deanna. So did I. I didn't want to listen to Deanna list all the reasons why Clue was going to lose!

Ashley and I rushed into the dog show's big backstage area and headed toward Clue's pen. A hundred smells and sounds hit us at once—dog shampoo, buzzing blow dryers, bubble bath, kids laughing, nail polish, dogs barking. It was great!

When we reached Clue's pen, I gasped. The pen was empty! Clue was gone!

"Clue has to be around somewhere," I said. "The door to the pen is open. She's probably just off exploring."

Ashley grabbed my arm. I could feel her fingers trembling. "Mary-Kate, Clue's leash is missing."

My stomach twisted. "Clue couldn't have put on her leash herself," I said.

Ashley nodded. Her blue eyes were wide and serious. "That means someone stole her!"